Civil War Ghosts

Read more of Daniel Cohen's
otherworldly tales:

Civil War Ghosts

Daniel Cohen

AN
APPLE
PAPERBACK

SCHOLASTIC INC.
New York Toronto London Auckland Sydney
Mexico City New Delhi Hong Kong

For Oliver,
who just showed up

Photo credits
1: "$100,000 reward! The murderer of our late beloved President, Abraham Lincoln, is still at large," Library of Congress LC-USZ62-11193-DLC; 2: "Incidents of the war. A harvest of death, Gettysburg, July, 1863," Library of Congress, LC-B8184-7964-A DLC; 3: "The assassination of President Lincoln: at Ford's Theatre, Washington, D.C., April 14th, 1865," Library of Congress, LC-USZ62-2073 DLC; 4: "Washington Navy Yard, D.C., Lewis Payne, the conspirator who attacked Secretary Seward, standing in overcoat and hat," Library of Congress, LC-B8171-7775 LC; 5: "Washington, D.C. Hanging bodies of the conspirators, guards only in yard," Library of Congress LC-B8171-1287; 6: "Andersonville Prison," Library of Congress LC-B8855-8216; 7: "Washington, D.C. The Old Capitol Prison, 1st and A Streets NE," Library of Congress LCB8171-1019LC; 8: "Portrait of Maj. Gen. Daniel E. Sickles, officer of the Federal Army," Library of Congress LC-B8172-1702 DLC.

Cover photos reproduced from the Collections of the Library of Congress.
Cover illustrated by Alicia Buelow.
Cover design by Ursula Albano.

ISBN 0-439-05387-0

12 11 10 9 8 7 6   4/0

Printed in the U.S.A.   40
First Scholastic printing, September 1999

CONTENTS

Introduction

GHOSTS IN GRAY AND BLUE

$\mathcal{T}$he Civil War was the bloodiest and most wrenching war ever fought in North America. It is also the most haunted period of American history.

What you will read about in the pages that follow is a series of Civil War ghostly encounters — I hesitate to call them "ghost stories." A "ghost story" is usually thought of as a tale that someone has made up to entertain, amaze, or frighten readers or listeners. Well, I didn't make up these stories. I only wish I had, for some of them are truly entertaining, amazing, and frightening.

These accounts of ghostly meetings have been

1

handed down over the years by people who experienced them and believed in them, or at least said that they believed in them.

I'm not going to swear to you that these are all "true" stories. People make mistakes, they exaggerate, they forget details, and they have an all-too-human tendency to see and hear what they think they should see and hear. To the frightened or overexcited imagination, the normal creaking of floorboards in an old house can sound like ghostly footsteps, a breeze rustling through trees can become the murmur of ghostly voices, and a swirl of fog can become a phantom.

And then people often do just make up things. Everybody likes to tell a good story, and a good story about ghosts is just about the best kind of story of all. And if it isn't true — well, what's the harm?

On the other hand, in most cases it isn't possible to prove that the stories are not true, either. Certainly the places, battlefields, forts, and prisons where these incidents are said to have taken place are real enough. So are the events, the battles, the assassinations, and the executions that inspired the tales. The history is all there. You can believe in the ghosts or not, as you wish.

I have also provided, whenever possible, addresses

and phone numbers for the places where the ghostly encounters are supposed to have taken place. You should be able to visit many of these places yourself. You may be lucky enough, or for the more timid among you, unlucky enough, to have your own ghostly encounter.

Chapter 1

HAUNTED BATTLEFIELDS

*M*any people believe that those whose lives have been cut short by violence are more likely to come back as ghosts. Their lives were unfulfilled and therefore their spirits are restless. Many people also believe that great and terrible events leave a "psychic impression" at the place where they occurred. Then, years later, this impression can become visible to particularly sensitive individuals.

Maybe for both of those reasons, scenes of great battles are often said to be haunted by the spirits of those who fought and died in the battle.

The earliest written accounts of haunted battlefields come from the Assyrians, who lived in biblical times. Later in history there are tales of ghosts being seen at a battlefield in Marathon, where in 490 B.C., the Greeks dealt a crushing blow to the invading Persians. It was said that those who visited the battlefield after sunset heard the clash of bronze and the screams of the wounded and dying — they even smelled the odor of blood. Even worse, anyone who saw the ghostly warriors was reportedly fated to die within a year. Marathon was not a place people felt comfortable about visiting after dark.

In England, there have been many reports of a ghostly reenactment of the battle of Edgehill. Fought on October 23, 1642, it was the first major battle of the English Civil War, and over a thousand men died that day.

As you might imagine, many battlefields of the American Civil War, the most deadly and most mythic war in the United States, are also supposed to be haunted.

The battle of Gettysburg, fought from July 1 to July 3, 1863, was a major turning point in the Civil War. The battle turned aside a Confederate attempt to invade the North. Partly because of the famous speech given there months later by President Abraham Lincoln, it is also the best-known battle of the war, and there are more ghostly tales attached to the Gettysburg battlefield than to any other Civil War site. Indeed, if even half the ghostly tales were to be credited, the battlefield today would be so crowded with phantoms that there would hardly be room for living visitors!

The ghostly associations began even before the battle itself. Here is an account that was often told during and just after the war:

The Union's Twentieth Maine Regiment, commanded by Colonel Joshua Chamberlain, had marched into Pennsylvania from Maryland. There they were told that the lines for a decisive battle were being drawn near the little town of Gettysburg. The weary men broke camp and marched on well into the night, hoping they were heading the right way. Then they came to what appeared to be an important fork in the road. They had no detailed maps, so they didn't know which way to go.

Suddenly there was a break in the clouds, and the moonlight shone down on a horseman wearing a bright coat and a three-cornered hat. Mounted on a magnificent horse, he galloped down one of the branching roads and waved for the men to follow.

Later Colonel Chamberlain described the event:

"At a turn of the road a staff officer, with an air of authority, told each colonel as he came up, 'General McClellan is in command again, and he's riding up ahead of us on the road.'

"Men waved their hats, cheered until they were hoarse, and wild with excitement, followed the figure on horseback. Although weary, they marched with miraculous enthusiasm believing their beloved general had returned to lead them into battle."

But it wasn't General McClellan, the former chief general of the Union Army. He was nowhere near Gettysburg. Then another rumor swept the ranks — the man on horseback was the spirit of George Washington himself. This inspired the tired and frightened men with even greater energy and confidence.

After arriving at the site of the battle, the Twentieth Maine was ordered to defend a partially wooded, boulder-strewn hill called Little Round Top. Their defense was to play a significant role in the ultimate outcome of the battle of Gettysburg.

As the battle developed, the Confederates, including the experienced and battle-hardened Fifteenth Alabama Regiment, were ordered to take Little Round Top at all costs. The Twentieth Maine was ordered to hold it at all costs. But the Confederate attackers outnumbered the Union defenders.

After hours of constant attack, the Twentieth Maine had very nearly run out of ammunition and the Confederates were still coming on strong. Their position seemed desperate, almost hopeless. Colonel Chamberlain reviewed his options and found that there were no good ones. He could not hold his position for much longer without ammunition, and he had been ordered not to withdraw. That left only attack. He thought that there was at least a small chance that a surprise attack might work. So Chamberlain shouted, "Fix bayonets! Charge!"

For a moment, no one moved. These were not professional soldiers. Not long before, they had been ordinary farmers and fishermen in Maine. Now they were being ordered to undertake what appeared to be a suicidal charge. Would they obey such an order?

Suddenly, or so the story goes, the mysterious figure appeared again, this time exhorting the men to follow him into battle. Inspired by the sight, the men of the Twentieth Maine plunged down the hill, thrusting their bayonets into the ranks of the bewildered

Confederates. The attack was so swift, so savage, and so unexpected that the Confederates did not have time to fire. They fell back in confusion. It was one of the most surprising turns of fortune in the entire war.

Many years later (and after he'd attained the rank of general), Joshua Chamberlain was interviewed about the story of the ghost of George Washington at Gettysburg.

The old soldier replied cautiously:

"Yes, that report was circulated through our lines, and I have no doubt that it inspired the men. Doubtless it was a superstition."

Then he paused and added,

"Who among us can say that such a thing was impossible? We have not yet sounded or explored the immortal life that lies out beyond the Bar.

"We do not know what mystic power may be possessed by those who are now bivouacking with the dead. I only know the effect, but I dare not explain or deny the cause. I do believe that we were enveloped by the powers of the other

9

world that day and who shall say that Washington was not among the number of those who aided the country he founded?"

In the battle of Gettysburg, General Robert E. Lee's Confederate Army was defeated. Both sides lost many men; the Confederates, however, were much less able to afford the losses. On July 4, 1863, Lee began a slow and agonizing retreat that continued well into the next day. Most of the Confederate wounded were carried in a seventeen-mile-long wagon train that rumbled down what is now Route 116 in Pennsylvania.

Many years later, Keith Tony, an historian and battlefield guide at the Gettysburg National Battlefield Military Park, was collecting accounts for a book that he was writing on battlefield ghosts. He admitted that he had never personally seen a ghost at Gettysburg. But one of his best eyewitness accounts came from his wife, Jill.

The Tonys lived in a house on the outskirts of the battlefield with a clear view of Route 116. The Fourth of July holiday, always a busy time at Gettysburg, was over. The mass of tourists had gone, and Jill Tony was looking forward to a few quiet days. At about two A.M., one of their children woke up screaming, apparently from a nightmare. After Jill quieted the child she went outside for a breath of air — it had been a hot night.

As she was standing in the doorway of her house, enjoying a cool breeze, she heard a low moaning sound coming from the area of the battlefield known as Seminary Ridge, where some of the key fighting had taken place. As the sound got louder, the moaning was punctuated by what sounded like cries of pain. And after that came some creaking sounds.

At first, Jill thought she was dreaming. Next she wondered if there had been an automobile accident, though she had not heard the screech of brakes or the unmistakable sound of metal crunching into metal. Then she saw where the noise was coming from.

There was a line of horse-drawn wagons coming slowly up Seminary Ridge and turning down Route 116. The moans and cries became more distinct, and soon she could make out the figures of men on horseback riding alongside the wagons, which appeared to be full of wounded men. Jill knew her history and she finally realized what she was seeing. It was the Confederate retreat from Gettysburg. She watched the scene for four or five minutes until the vision of the wagon train simply disappeared.

Was it a hallucination? The wife of a battlefield guide would certainly know all the details of the retreat. Maybe she had gone back to bed and simply dreamed she had seen the wagons. Some dreams can be very realistic, and it is often hard to separate them from reality. But later Jill talked about her experience with others in the town. She spoke carefully at first, because if you say you have seen ghosts, many people tend to think that you are crazy. Much to her surprise, however, she discovered that others had had similar experiences. They, too, had witnessed the ghostly retreat.

Oddly, no witness has ever reported seeing the spectral Confederate wagon train a second time. Tony speculated, "Perhaps the wagons roll only once for their human audience."

While people throughout history have reported seeing phantom armies reenact battles on battlefields, a phantom battle in the ballroom of a mansion is strange even in the strange realm of ghostly tales. Yet it is said that this happens in an historic and beautifully restored mansion in the French Quarter of New Orleans.

The house was built in the 1820s and is now known as the Beauregard-Keyes house after its two most famous owners, Confederate General Pierre Gustave Toutant Beauregard and twentieth-century novelist Frances Parkinson Keyes. It is General Beauregard in whom we are interested in here.

Beauregard had come from a very prominent New Orleans family. He was in command of the Confederate forces that fired on Fort Sumter on April 12, 1861, the event that marked the start of the Civil War. Then, a year later, he led his troops at the battle of Shiloh on April 6–7, 1862. Nearly 20,100 men lost their lives.

After the war, Beauregard retired to the mansion in New Orleans. Since then there have been mysterious reports that in some way his wartime experiences followed him there.

Today the restored mansion is a popular inn and tourist attraction where guests are entertained by guides in period costume. At night, however, things may be different. It has been said that on some nights there is a ghostly reenactment of the battle of Shiloh in the mansion's ballroom. The walls of the room appear to fade and open out into a scene of the Shiloh battleground as it was in 1862. General Beauregard, astride a great white horse, enters the scene through the ballroom's enormous double doors.

The battle begins and wears on through the

night — and as time passes the scene becomes more grisly and more terrifying. Then, as the light of dawn breaks, the battle scene fades and disappears completely.

Though the story of the ghostly battle in the mansion has been repeated often, its origin is impossible to pin down. It has been said that a great number of people have witnessed the scene — but we don't know the names of any of the witnesses. Many others who have not seen the battle say they can feel its anguish, despair, and violence when they enter the ballroom.

One person who doesn't buy into any of these tales is Marion Chambon, director of the Beauregard-Keyes house. She has spent a great deal of time in the house and has never seen the phantom battle. Still, she does admit the old place can feel a bit scary at times, particularly at night.

She does not rule out the possibility of ghosts in the mansion but insists if there are any ghosts around they are happy ones. She then goes on to tell another ghost story associated with the house. After the war, General Beauregard became an official of the Louisiana government. At one point, he and his wife made extensive plans for a very elegant ball to be held in his home. Then, just a few days before it was to take place, Beauregard was called away on urgent business and the ball had to be canceled.

However, New Orleans party-goers are hard to discourage. It is said that every once in a while the ghosts of long-dead guests gather in the grand ballroom to have the ball that they were denied in life.

A great battle or a grand ball? Take your choice.

Of the many great and terrible battles of the Civil War, Antietam may have been the worst. On a single day, September 17, 1862, nearly twenty-three thousand men were either killed, wounded, or missing. It was the single bloodiest day of battle in all of American history.

One of the best-known and most colorful units in the Union Army was the Irish Brigade. Commanded by Brigadier General Thomas Meagher, it had been recruited largely from among Irish immigrants in New York. By the time of the battle of Antietam, the Irish Brigade had been reinforced by troops who were not Irish, but still they all marched under a green battle flag bearing the symbol of an Irish harp.

During the battle, the Irish Brigade was chosen to make a dangerous attack on a Confederate stronghold. As they advanced, the men of the brigade raised an old Irish war chant, *"Faugh-a-Ballagh! Faugh-a-*

Ballagh! Faugh-a-Ballagh!" Pronounced fah-lah-ba-LAH, it can be roughly translated as "Get out of the way!"

Despite the chilling war cry, more than half the men in the Irish Brigade were either killed or wounded by the end of the day.

Now fast forward to the 1990s. A group of Baltimore middle schoolers was visiting Antietam National Battlefield in Maryland. The park rangers showed them a short film about the battle and then gave them a tour of the battlefield. At one point during the tour, the group split up, and some of the students wandered over to the area where the Irish Brigade had made its futile charge.

Later, when all of the students had gathered together again, those who had wandered off asked their guide about some singing they had heard. Some members of the group said it sounded more like men chanting. Most, however, said it was singing — and strangely enough they said it sounded like a Christmas carol, or at least like part of one, repeated over and over again (which was completely unexpected in the middle of a warm spring afternoon). Though some of the sounds were quite loud and close, the students were not able to see the men who were making them. They even wondered if the singing could have come from some sort of hidden loudspeaker.

The guide said that at this point the hair on the back of his neck was standing up. He asked the students to tell him exactly what they heard. The best they could come up with was "Fa-la-la-la-lah," the refrain from the Christmas carol "Deck the Halls."

"Did it sound more like "Fah-lah-ba-LAH?" the guide asked.

"That's it!" cried the students. "How did you know?"

The guide swears that there was no way a group of ordinary Baltimore students could have known about anything as obscure as the war chant used by the Irish Brigade at that exact spot on the battlefield 130 years earlier. And there was nothing about it in the film or presentation given to the students before their Antietam battlefield tour.

There have been other reports of strange and unusual sounds on the Antietam battlefield — but none as unusual or striking as the cry of *"Faugh-a-Ballagh!"*

Where to Go

Please call the sites for directions and visiting hours.

Antietam National Battlefield
Route 65
Sharpsburg, Maryland
(301) 432-5124

Beauregard-Keyes House
1113 Chartres St.
New Orleans, Louisiana 70116
(504) 523-7257

Gettysburg National Military Park
96 Taneytown Road
Gettysburg, Pennsylvania
(717) 334-1124

Shiloh National Military Park
1055 Pittsburg Landing
Shiloh, Tennessee
(901) 689-5696

Chapter 2

THE HAUNTS OF MARY SURRATT

*T*he single most dramatic event of the Civil War took place less than a week after the war officially ended.

On April 9, 1865, General Robert E. Lee surrendered to General Ulysses S. Grant at Appomattox Court House, Virginia.

On April 14, the actor John Wilkes Booth crept into the presidential box at Ford's Theater in Washington, D.C, and fired a single shot into the head of President Abraham Lincoln. The assassin then jumped from the box and injured his leg by catching his heel in the bunting that decorated the box. Still, he was able to run across the stage, out a back door, and into an alley where an accomplice was waiting with a horse so Booth could make his escape.

The gravely wounded Lincoln was carried to a house across the street from the theater; he died there a few hours later.

Booth was no lone gunman, but the leader of a conspiracy of Southern sympathizers. Around the same time that Booth shot the President, Louis Powell (sometimes known as Louis Paine or Payne) broke into the house of Secretary of State William H. Seward, attacking him with a knife and nearly killing him. Another conspirator, George Atzerodt, was stalking Vice President Andrew Johnson — but he lost his nerve, got drunk, and didn't attempt the planned assassination.

The plot was clumsy and ill-conceived, and it unraveled quickly. Many of the conspirators were rounded up within hours. Booth and his associate David Herold were able to escape their pursuers for twelve days. They were finally trapped in a barn on Garrett's Farm near Bowling Green, Virginia. Herold surrendered. The barn was then set on fire in an attempt to drive Booth out, but before that could happen, he was fatally shot by Sergeant Boston Corbett, though there had been orders to take him alive. Some believe Booth actually shot himself.

Justice was swift in those days. The conspirators were brought to trial and convicted in a matter of weeks: Four of them were sentenced to hang. The sentence was carried out on July 7, 1865, on a scaffold erected on the grounds of the old Arsenal Penitentiary, near Capitol Hill.

There has never been any doubt about the guilt of three of those who were executed—Powell, Herold, and Atzerodt. But the attitude has been different toward the fourth person who was hanged on July 7. Her name was Mary Surratt.

One reason for the difference in attitude is that Mary Surratt was a woman.

But there is also a possibility that Mary Surratt was unjustly sentenced to death. The chief evidence against her was that the plotters often met at her Washington, D.C., boardinghouse and that her son, John, was deeply involved in the conspiracy.

During the trial and right up to the time she was executed, Mary always protested her innocence. She said that while Booth had visited the boardinghouse often enough, she barely knew him and had no idea of what he and the others were planning.

And even if Mary knew more than she ever admitted, there is the question of the fairness of her sentence. Not all of those captured and convicted were sentenced to death. Mary's son, John Surratt, for example, escaped to Canada and then to Europe after the assassination. He was recognized and arrested two years later and sent back to the United States for trial. But by that time, passions had cooled, and though he had been one of the central figures in the plot to kill Lincoln, he (unlike his mother) was given a relatively light sentence.

A woman who was involved in the most sensational crime of nineteenth-century America and who may have been executed unjustly is certainly the stuff of ghostly legend. And, sure enough, Mary Surratt's ghost and ghostly influence have been seen and felt in many places.

Mary Surratt originally came from Maryland. She and her husband, John, ran a twelve-hundred-acre farm about thirteen miles south of Washington. As the region became more populated, they turned part of their home into a general store and tavern that became the central gathering place for the area. The region even became known as Surrattsville — a name that was changed to Clinton, Maryland, immediately after her execution.

When her husband died, Mary leased the Maryland property to John Lloyd, a former Washington policeman turned tavernkeeper. Then she and her two children moved to Washington, where she ran a boardinghouse.

The Surratt family visited the inn regularly and remained on friendly terms with Lloyd, though he was to testify against Mary later.

Over the years the old tavern had many owners, reportedly including Edwin Booth, the assassin's brother and a very famous actor. The inn's association with Mary Surratt and the Lincoln assassination might have been completely forgotten were it not for a series of strange and ghostly happenings.

There have been reports of muffled voices and mumblings in the old building. No one who has heard these sounds has ever been able to make out the words, but most have assumed they are the voices of the plotters, still whispering to one another long after their deaths.

A more striking manifestation is the figure of a woman in a long black Civil War–era dress, often seen on the tavern's porch. The figure is said to be Mary Surratt herself. Perhaps she is revisiting the place where she spent her happiest days, or perhaps she is looking for John Lloyd, the man whose testimony may have sealed her fate.

The Surratt boardinghouse in Washington is said to be haunted, too. After Mary's execution, it became the property of her daughter, Anna. It was not a popular piece of property, and Anna Surratt was eventually forced to sell it at a greatly reduced price. After that, no one seemed willing or able to own the house for long, and one new owner followed another in such rapid succession that the house again attracted the attention of Washington journalists.

These reporters found former owners who spoke of "mumblings" and "muffled voices" much like those reported at the Surratt tavern in Maryland. Some claimed they could hear the details of the assassination plot being discussed by the ghostly voices.

From the back room (once Mary's bedroom) came the sound of ghostly footsteps. It was said that Mary's ghost was doomed to walk Washington for eternity, or at least until her name was cleared.

The old boardinghouse has been renovated so many times that it bears almost no resemblance to its original Civil War appearance. At one point, it became an Asian grocery store. In recent decades, owners have insisted that they have heard no ghostly voices or footsteps. But of course, if the place had a reputation for being haunted, that might hurt its resale price. It certainly has done so in the past — and ghosts are the sort of thing that property owners are usually very reluctant to discuss.

After her arrest, Mary Surratt was taken to the Old Brick Capitol. This building served briefly as the Capitol and was converted into a prison during the Civil War. In the early years of the twentieth century, the Old Brick Capitol was torn down to make room for the new Supreme Court building. But before it was destroyed, on the anniversary of Mary Surratt's execution, a female figure was seen against one of the windows. Witnesses reported that the figure sobbed incessantly while clenching her "ghostly white fists against black iron bars." The apparition was said to be Mary Surratt. The ghostly sobs were also heard regularly by those who worked in the building.

On the evening before her execution, Mary Surratt's daughter, Anna, forced her way inside the White House grounds and made it as far as the front door, where she pleaded for the life of her mother. On the anniversary of that night, some claim to have seen Anna's spirit banging on the front door of the White House, pleading once again for Mary's release.

Ever since her hanging on July 7, 1865, the ghost of Mary Surratt has been reported haunting the Arsenal grounds.

The bodies of the conspirators were buried near the

gallows but later moved to permanent graves. There is a tale that Mary Surratt's spirit somehow influenced the mysterious growth of a boxwood tree on the site where the scaffold once stood. According to the legend, this is just one more way the restless ghost has tried to attract attention and prove her innocence.

The death sentence on Mary Surratt and the other three conspirators was pronounced by Judge Advocate General Joseph Holt. Holt has never been a particularly popular figure in history. He was taciturn and ill-mannered and made few friends. After the conspiracy trial he became a virtual recluse. He is said to have locked himself in his house and spent most of his time rereading the transcripts of the famous trial. After he died, the new owners of the house claimed that they heard his remorseful spirit pacing up and down in his room for hours on end.

When the house was finally torn down, Judge Holt's spirit, wearing a midnight-blue Union uniform with his cape wrapped tightly around him, was seen walking down First Street. The legend says that he was on his way to the Old Brick Capitol to question Mary Surratt once again.

Oddly, while there are many tales and legends associated with chief conspirator and assassin John Wilkes Booth (including the most persistent, that he was not shot at Garrett's farm), none of them involve his ghost. There is, however, one odd little legend.

After shooting the President, Booth jumped from the presidential box and ran across the stage to make his escape. It is believed that any actors who attempt to speak their lines along the route across the stage taken by Booth will become hopelessly muddled.

Where to Go

The Old Washington Arsenal Penitentiary was located on the grounds of Fort Leslie McNair, not too far from Capitol Hill. The gallows was in the courtyard on the northern end of the fort. Mary Surratt's much-renovated former boardinghouse is at 694 H Street NW. Ford's Theater, now beautifully restored to its Civil War glory, is one of Washington's top tourist attractions. And if you stand in front of the White House on the evening of July 6, you might just catch a glimpse of the ghost of Anna Surratt, still banging on the front door in a futile attempt to save her mother's life.

However, if you happen to be looking for the grave of assassin John Wilkes Booth, you are out of luck. It is probably an unmarked grave in Green Mount Cemetery in Baltimore, Maryland. But other reports hold that the body was buried near the old

Washington, D.C., jail (where all traces of the grave have been obliterated), dumped into the Potomac River, or secretly buried on an island twenty-seven miles from the capital.

Please call the sites for directions and visiting hours.

Ford's Theater
511 10th Street NW
Washington, D.C.
(202) 426-6924

Supreme Court
First Street and Maryland Avenue NE
Washington, D.C.
(202) 479-3000

Surratt House Museum
9118 Brandywine Road
Clinton, Maryland
(301) 868-1121

White House
1600 Pennsylvania Avenue NW
Washington, D.C.
(202) 456-1414

Chapter 3

THE MANY GHOSTS OF ABRAHAM LINCOLN

*N*obody in American history has been more associated with ghost stories and legends than Abraham Lincoln, who was President throughout the Civil War.

Inevitably, any death as tragic, dramatic, and historically important as that of Abraham Lincoln is bound to inspire ghostly tales. But in the case of Lincoln there was much more involved.

Most significantly there was the movement called Spiritualism. Spiritualism began in upstate New York in the late 1840s. In a very few years it had spread, not only throughout the United States but throughout much of the Western world. (And it's still with us today, though it is not nearly as popular and influential as it was in the past.)

Spiritualist belief holds that the dead can communicate with the living with the aid of a uniquely gifted person called a medium. This communication is supposed to take place during a special meeting or gathering called a seance. Spiritualism and seances can bring great comfort to those who have recently lost loved ones. It's not surprising, then, that there have been upsurges of interest in spiritualist beliefs during times of war — like the Civil War or World War I.

There is absolutely no evidence to suggest that Abraham Lincoln himself was a spiritualist. But we cannot be so sure about his wife. Mary Todd Lincoln was a deeply unhappy, deeply troubled woman whose life was scarred by tragedy. Not only was her husband shot while she sat beside him, but three of her four children died before she did. Only Robert Todd Lincoln lived to be an adult. Edward died a month before his fourth birthday, before Lincoln became President. Tad outlived his father by only six years. And Willie's death was the most tragic of all. He died of fever halfway through his father's first term when he was only eleven years old.

Next to the President himself, the ghost of young Willie has been reported most often in the White House. A member of the staff of President Ulysses S. Grant said that he had actually conversed with the boy's ghost.

Willie may have been the family favorite, and the little boy's unexpected death had a profound impact on both the President and his wife. Lincoln used to spend hours sitting in the boy's crypt in Washington. And Mary Todd Lincoln, her fragile hold on reality nearly shattered, eventually turned to spiritualist mediums for comfort.

The President's wife invited spiritualist mediums to the White House for seances, and newspaper accounts indicate that the President himself attended some of them. On April 23, 1863, the *Chicago Tribune* reported that Lincoln was at a White House seance conducted by medium Charles Shockle and was very impressed by what took place. Pictures on the wall swayed, candlesticks rose into the air, tables moved, and mysterious rapping sounds were heard.

A truly remarkable White House seance was supposed to have been conducted by a medium named Mrs. Miller. During the seance, the medium placed her hand on top of a big grand piano and it rose into the air. Then Lincoln invited the Honorable D. E.

Somes (a weighty former congressman from Maine) and another substantial fellow to sit on top of the piano. "I think we can hold this instrument down," the President reportedly said. The added weight made no difference, and the piano rose again at the medium's touch.

There are grimmer stories like the celebrated account of Lincoln's prophetic dream of his own death. One of the President's close friends, Ward Hill Lamon, wrote an account of what Lincoln had said to him on an evening early in 1865.

Lincoln described a dream he had had a few days earlier. In it, Lincoln heard sobbing, got out of bed, and wandered downstairs to see what had happened. He went into the East Room, where he saw a platform on which rested a coffin containing a corpse whose face was covered. Around the platform were soldiers and a throng of people, some staring at the corpse, others weeping.

As Lamon described the incident, Lincoln said: "'Who is dead in the White House?' I demanded of one of the soldiers. 'The President,' was his answer. 'He was killed by an assassin.'"

There are a couple of problems with this story. The greatest of them is that Lamon didn't begin telling the tale until several years after Lincoln had been assassinated and after the legends had begun to accumulate around the murdered President!

But is it so remarkable that Abraham Lincoln would have dreamed of being assassinated? His life was threatened regularly, and several unsuccessful attempts on his life had actually been made. He once had a bullet pass through his celebrated top hat. Abraham Lincoln was always aware of the possibility of assassination yet was notoriously careless about his personal safety. He didn't need the gift of prophecy to dream of the possibility that he would be killed. He knew that was one of the hazards of his position, and he accepted it without complaint.

Still, the story has become an integral part of the Lincoln legend.

There is another part to the Lincoln legend, the appearance of his ghost in the White House. Many ghosts have been reported at 1600 Pennsylvania Avenue. For instance, John Adams was the first President to occupy the White House (before it was even completed) and the ghost of his wife, Abigail, has been spotted hanging out her washing in the East Room. Dolley Madison, the high-spirited wife of President James Madison, has been seen there, too, as has President Andrew Jackson — and Thomas Jefferson has been heard playing his violin. But the ghost most closely associated with the White House is Abraham Lincoln's.

Perhaps President Theodore Roosevelt was only speaking figuratively when he said, "I think of Lincoln, shambling, homely, with his sad, strong, deeply furrowed face, all of the time. I see him in the different rooms and in the halls."

But Grace Coolidge, wife of President Calvin Coolidge, described actually seeing Lincoln, dressed "in black, with a stole draped across his shoulders to ward off the drafts and chills of Washington's night air." He was looking out of a window in the Oval Office — a window that the melancholy President often gazed out of during the dark days of the Civil War.

Lincoln's ghost seems to have been unusually active during the administration of President Franklin D. Roosevelt. Eleanor Roosevelt, the President's wife, said that while she had never seen the ghost herself, she had often felt Lincoln's presence. She also related a story told by one of her secretaries, who passed the Lincoln bedroom and saw a lanky figure sitting on the bed, pulling on his boots. A newspaper account of the time tells of FDR's valet running screaming from the White House into the arms of a guard, shouting that he had just seen the ghost of Lincoln.

And Roosevelt's famous Scottish terrier, Fala,

would often bark at something that no one else could see. People often remarked that the dog must be barking at a ghost.

Many White House visitors have also encountered the ghost of the sixteenth President. Queen Wilhelmina of The Netherlands was staying at the White House during the Roosevelt Administration when, late one evening, she heard a knock at the door. There, right in front of her, filling most of the doorway, was the tall, top-hatted figure of Abraham Lincoln. The shocked queen simply fainted.

Winston Churchill, the British Prime Minister, stayed at the White House many times during World War II. The Lincoln bedroom was traditionally where visiting male heads of state were lodged. Churchill, however, hated the room and often slept in the room across the hall. He never explained why he had such an aversion to the Lincoln bedroom.

Roosevelt's successor, Harry Truman, never saw any ghosts. However, he did recall that in the early morning hours a little over a year after he became President, he was awakened by two loud and distinct knocks on the door of his bedroom. He got up, went to the door, and opened it. But all he found was a cold spot that went away and mysterious footsteps that trailed off down the corridor.

Later, after he left Washington, Truman told his daughter, Bess, he could never understand why Lincoln or anyone else would want to haunt the White House, saying, "No man in his right mind would want to go there of his own accord."

Susan Ford, the daughter of President Gerald Ford, once told an interviewer for *Seventeen* magazine that she believed in ghosts and would never sleep in the Lincoln bedroom. It must be noted, however, that in recent times none of the many, many visitors to the Lincoln bedroom have complained about being bothered by ghosts.

Sightings of Lincoln's ghost at the White House have declined since the Truman Administration. Since that time, too, the White House has undergone extensive and much needed renovations, which have changed it drastically from the way it was in Lincoln's day. Perhaps the ghost no longer feels comfortable there!

For years after Lincoln's death he was a favorite figure for spiritualist mediums. Scores of them reported receiving messages from the dead President. A large number of "spirit photographs" of Lincoln still exist today. The most famous of them is a photograph of Mary Todd Lincoln seated at a table with a semitransparent, ghostly image of Abraham Lincoln hovering in the background. Spirit photographs are supposed to show a spirit or ghost. It hardly seems necessary to point out that such photographs are fakes. They look obvious and crude to us today, but back in the middle of the nineteenth century, when photography was still a novelty, they fooled a lot of people.

Sightings of Lincoln's ghost have also been reported at the Lincoln Memorial in Washington and at Lincoln's tomb in Springfield, Illinois, the place Lincoln called home. There are even rumors that Lincoln's body was stolen and is not really buried in Springfield at all.

After Lincoln's death, his body was taken aboard a special train to his native Illinois for burial. All along the route, mourners lined the tracks to see the funeral train pass. And this has led to one of the most enduring ghostly legends attached to Abraham Lincoln — the legend of the phantom or ghost train.

Ever since 1865, according to this legend, a ghostly funeral train takes the same route at the same time in April year after year. The train is covered in black bunting and the engine is manned by skeletons. On one of the flat cars that follows the engine, a skeleton band plays soundlessly.

This description appeared in *The Albany Evening Times*:

"It passes noiselessly. If it is moonlight, clouds come over the moon as the phantom train goes by. After the pilot engine passes, the funeral train itself with flags and streamers rushes past. The track seems covered with black carpet, and the coffin is seen in the center of the car, while all about it in the air and on the train behind are vast numbers of blue-coated men, some with coffins on their backs, others leaning upon them."

According to the legend, all the clocks stop as the train passes and it is five to eight minutes before they resume again.

In 1959, New York historian and folklorist Louis C. Jones wrote, "It must be that the eyes of men are no longer as keen as they used to be, for there are only a few of the old-timers left who know why one day each April all the trains are late."

Where to Go
The public sections of the White House are open to visitors, but be sure to call for updated information

on tours. Your representative in Congress may also be able to help you arrange a White House tour if you contact his or her office.

Please call the sites for directions and visiting hours.

Abraham Lincoln Tomb
W. Monument Ave.
Springfield, Illinois
(217) 782-2717

Lincoln Memorial
West Potomac Park at 23rd Street NW
Washington, D.C.
(202) 426-6841

White House
1600 Pennsylvania Avenue NW
Washington, D.C.
(202) 456-1414

Chapter 4

THE GHOSTLY CIRCLE

*T*he circle of ghostly tales and legends surrounding the Lincoln assassination is enormous. It takes in not only the murdered President and the assassination plotters, but also many who were less directly connected with the terrible event.

Take the case of Dr. Samuel Mudd, for instance. After John Wilkes Booth shot Lincoln, Booth and David Herold fled from Washington into Maryland. Booth had injured his leg jumping from the President's box, so at four in the morning of April 15, 1865, he and Herold knocked on the door of Dr.

Mudd's farmhouse in Charles County, Maryland, about three miles from Beantown.

Dr. Mudd treated Booth's leg, and Booth and Herold rested at the house until the afternoon. Several days later, Dr. Mudd was arrested for his suspected role in the Lincoln assassination. Mudd protested his innocence, claiming that while he had met Booth in the past, he did not recognize the actor when he stopped for treatment because he was wearing a disguise. But federal authorities had reason to doubt his claim. Dr. Mudd was a known Confederate sympathizer.

Dr. Mudd was tried and convicted by a military court and sentenced to life imprisonment at Fort Jefferson on Dry Tortugas Island, Florida. In less than four years, he was pardoned and released from prison by President Andrew Johnson, but his conviction was not overturned. His release was supported by the other prisoners and guards in the prison in appreciation for Dr. Mudd's services during a yellow fever epidemic that swept the island.

Dr. Mudd returned to his home in Maryland in March 1869, but both his health and reputation had been shattered. He died in 1883.

Historians have argued about Dr. Mudd's complicity in the assassination plot. Mudd's supporters, most notably members of his family, have worked long and hard to clear their ancestor's name. In the fall of 1998, a federal judge even ordered the U.S. Army (Mudd was convicted by a military court) to reconsider his conviction. No final legal settlement of the case is in sight, however.

Louise Mudd Arehart, the last member of the Mudd family to be born in the old farmhouse, has worked to clear the family name and spent a lot of time restoring and preserving the Mudd family farmhouse as an historically significant landmark. She also says that the ghost of her long-dead grandfather has encouraged her in this effort.

The ghost did not appear to her at the original family home, which was abandoned and falling apart at the time. Instead, it came to her in her own house in La Plata, Maryland.

At first, there were all the usual ghostly signs: unexplained knockings and footsteps, doors that opened and closed mysteriously. But soon the ghostly figure itself put in an appearance. It was a man dressed in black trousers, a vest, and a white shirt with sleeves rolled up to the elbow. At the beginning Mrs. Arehart only saw the figure outside of the house, but later it entered the house itself. Once Louise Arehart almost ran into the phantom while going through a doorway into the dining room! The house was thoroughly searched, but no physical trace of the mysterious intruder was ever found.

Though she never saw the face of the unknown visitor clearly, Louise was convinced that she was seeing the ghost of her grandfather Dr. Samuel Mudd. There had never been previous reports of such a ghost in her house. Why had Dr. Mudd decided to appear after all those years? Louise thought she knew the reason — he had come back to find someone who would help preserve the old family home. Louise Arehart took on the task with a great deal of energy and not only raised the money to begin restoration on the house but also arranged to have it listed on the National Register of Historic Places. It is now open to the public. The ghost of Dr. Samuel Mudd, apparently deciding that his task on earth was now complete, has not been seen there since.

Perhaps he will be back to celebrate if his family finally has his conviction overturned.

Among those seated in President Lincoln's box on the night that he was shot were Major Henry Reed Rathbone, a brilliant and successful young officer, and his fiancée, Clara Harris, of Albany, New York, the daughter of U.S. Senator Ira Harris. When the assassin fired, Major Rathbone lunged for him. Booth's pistol contained only one shot. But the assassin also carried a knife, and he slashed Rathbone's arm, creating a large gash from the shoulder to the elbow.

Major Rathbone recovered from his physical injuries, but his mind never seemed to recover from the events of that terrible night. He became moody and distracted. He still married Clara Harris on July 11, 1867. She accepted his moods and hoped that, in time, he would become his old self again; that never happened.

The major's army career became increasingly difficult for him. He resigned his commission and moved to Germany, since he came from a wealthy family and could live where he wished. His wife, Clara, hoped that the change of scene would help, but it didn't. If anything, Rathbone became moodier and more depressed.

One evening in 1883, as Rathbone's wife and children prepared for a Christmas visit to America, Major Rathbone took a pistol and shot his wife to death. He probably would have killed his children, too, if their nurse had not stopped him. Finally, Rathbone tried to kill himself, but once again he recovered from his wounds. Major Rathbone spent the rest of his life in an insane asylum. (He died in 1911.)

As word of the Rathbone tragedy reached Washington, people began to shun the house where the major had lived at the time of the Lincoln assassination. They feared that somehow the web of violence that had touched so many who had been associated with the assassination might somehow curse the house. And there were reports of the sound of a man crying coming from the empty house.

Clara Harris Rathbone was well remembered in her hometown of Albany, New York. She returned there before she married Major Rathbone, and she was tortured by the memory of the night of the assassination. The white satin dress she wore that night was spattered with the blood of Abraham Lincoln as well as with the blood of her future husband. Of course, she could never wear the dress again. Yet she could not bring herself to dispose of it, either. It hung by itself in her closet.

After she married, and Clara and her husband went to live in Washington and later Germany, there was considerable discussion about what should be done with the dress. She didn't want to take the dress with her, but she still didn't want to destroy it. It was widely believed that she had hidden the dress somewhere in her Albany home — though no one knew where.

This popular Albany legend was later used as the basis for a short story called "The White Satin Dress." The story was about the people who occupied the house after Clara Harris left. They were related to a governor of Massachusetts, who visited them regularly. During one visit, the governor was brooding over a difficult political decision he had to make. If he made the unpopular decision, it would probably cost him reelection — yet he was convinced that the unpopular decision was the correct one for the welfare of his state.

The conflict disturbed his sleep, and at one point he awakened with a start, sure that someone was in the room with him. In the moonlight he thought he saw the figure of Abraham Lincoln — and then it was gone. When he got up to turn on the light, he knocked a volume of Lincoln's speeches off a nightstand by his bed. The volume fell open and the governor's eyes were drawn to the words, "Hew honestly to the line; let the Lord take care of the chips." The governor then determined to make the unpopular but correct decision. (That fall, to his great surprise, he was reelected anyway.)

The governor told his hosts of his experience in the guest bedroom. They were sure it was the product of a tired and overwrought mind. But later, when they had some renovations done in the house, workers found a tiny closet in the guest room. It had been completely sealed off and forgotten. And in the closet hung the white satin dress that was stained with Lincoln's blood.

Finally there is the tangled little tale of the angry husband, the missing leg, and the foiled assassination.

It's important to understand that in many ways nineteenth-century Washington was a small town. Everybody who worked in or around the government pretty much knew everybody else who worked in or around the government.

Daniel Sickles had been a congressman from New York, a Foreign Service officer in London, a close campaign aide of pre-Civil War President James Buchanan, and then a congressman again.

Congressman Sickles and his young wife, Theresa, lived in a fine home on Lafayette Street and were at the very center of Washington's social scene.

With all his political activities, Sickles didn't have too much time for his wife. Left alone, she soon found companionship with another man, Philip Barton Key (son of Francis Scott Key, who composed the national anthem). Key was a widower, but was still a handsome and vigorous man who was popular with the ladies.

Since Washington was such a small town, the affair between Key and Mrs. Sickles was well-known to Washington gossips. But Sickles himself knew nothing, until someone sent him an anonymous letter describing in detail what was going on. Sickles angrily confronted his wife; she broke down and confessed.

As the days passed, Sickles became more and more distraught. He went about muttering that he was a ruined and dishonored man. Then, about a week after learning of the affair, Sickles saw Key walk past his house on his way to the fashionable Washington Club. Sickles thought he saw Key try to signal his wife, and that was the last straw. "My God, this is horrible!" he shouted as he grabbed two pistols and went in search of Key.

Sickles waited in front of the Washington Club and when he saw Key come out he called, "Key, you scoundrel, you have dishonored my house — you must die!" He fired one pistol and wounded Key slightly. Terrified, Key began backing up toward the Washington Club, but Sickles produced his second pistol, and this time he fired at point-blank range. Key didn't have a chance.

Sickles was arrested for the murder. He hired the best lawyers, and after a sensational trial, he was acquitted on the grounds of "temporary aberration of mind." (It was the first time such a plea had ever been used successfully in the United States.) The Washington jury may have been a bit wary of convicting so prominent and influential a man; there was also a general view that husbands had a "right" to avenge their honor by killing their rivals.

Many people reported seeing Key's restless spirit in the vicinity of the Washington Club where he had been shot. In fact, Key became one of Washington's best-known ghosts — but not a Civil War ghost — not yet!

By the time of the Civil War, the old Washington Club had closed and the building had become the home of Secretary of State William H. Seward. It was quite near his State Department office. Apparently the Seward family did not worry about the ghost tales — there were far more dangerous things in Washington during the war.

On April 14, 1865, John Wilkes Booth and his associates wanted to do more than just kill President Lincoln — they wanted to disrupt the entire government. This part of the plot went seriously awry, though a second assassination attempt that night very nearly succeeded. Former Confederate soldier Louis Powell was to kill Secretary of State William H. Seward. At the time, Seward was recovering from injuries he had received in a serious carriage accident and was completely incapable of defending himself. However, when Powell broke into the Seward house, there was a great deal of noise. This alerted Seward's son, Frederick, and a servant, who were then able to rush to the secretary's defense and save him from the knife-wielding Powell. Had it not been for the noises, the Secretary of State would surely have been killed.

Where did the noises come from? Some have said that Powell was clumsy, but many more believe that the ghost of Philip Barton Key, sensing another tragedy, made the noises that averted the assassination. Key may have been a cad, but even in death he was a patriot.

Now remember the vengeful Daniel Sickles. After he was acquitted of murder, his political career continued with hardly a pause. When the Civil War broke out, he raised his own contingent of men from the state of New York, and was eventually awarded the rank of general. He was sometimes invited to dine at the White House with the Lincoln family.

At the battle of Gettysburg, General Sickles was wounded and his leg had to be amputated. He regarded the loss of a leg as a badge of courage and patriotism, and he personally bequeathed his severed leg to the Army Medical Museum. After the war, Sickles sometimes took friends to the museum to show them his preserved, severed leg and regale them with stories of his valor.

When Sickles died, so the stories go, he retained his affection for that leg even from beyond the grave. One custodian of the museum reported encountering "a fat shadow, with one leg, that seemed to float" near the glass case in which the leg was displayed. In his later years, Sickles had become quite fat. Others who worked in the museum reported similar experiences, always at night when the museum building was closed to visitors.

The Army Medical Museum is now known as the National Museum of Health and Medicine of the Armed Forces Institute of Pathology. The Hirshorn

Museum now stands where the old museum once was. No corpulent one-legged ghosts have been reported in either location. The general's severed leg is still on display.

Where to Go
Please call the sites for directions and visiting hours.

Dr. Samuel A. Mudd House and Museum
Waldorf, Maryland
(301) 934-8464 or (301) 645-6870

National Museum of Health and Medicine of the Armed Forces Institute of Pathology
Walter Reed Army Medical Center
6825 16th Street NW
Washington, D.C.
(202) 782-2672

Chapter 5

GHOSTS AT THE FORTRESS

*T*he earliest colonists recognized the strategic importance of the spit of land between the James and York Rivers in Virginia. They named it Point Comfort because of its sheltered harbor, and the first fortifications were built there as early as 1608.

After that there were a succession of fortifications built on the spot — the last and largest was Fort Monroe, which was completed in 1834.

Captain John Smith, of Pocahontas fame, commented that Point Comfort would be a fine place for a castle. And that's what Fort Monroe resembled when it was built. Designed by a former aide to

Napoleon, the fort would not have looked out of place in medieval Europe.

It is the only fort in America completely surrounded by a moat. It is also surrounded by a thick stone wall. The wall encompasses an area of sixty-three acres dominated by three military-style stone buildings and a large number of homes for the members of the garrison and their families.

At the start of the Civil War, Fort Monroe was considered the strongest fort in America. It was controlled by Union Forces. Despite its strategic location in Virginia, a Confederate state, the Confederacy decided it was too strong to attack, though they certainly would like to have captured it, for the fort served as a base for a number of important Union operations in Virginia and along the coast.

A structure as old, prominent, and forbidding as Fort Monroe would seem to be a perfect place for ghosts. And so it has proven to be. If all the stories are true, Fort Monroe has been the gathering place for a virtual Who's Who of American ghosts. Captain John Smith has been seen there; so has the Marquis de Lafayette, a Frenchman who was a major general in the American Revolution. One of America's most well-traveled specters, that of writer Edgar

Allan Poe, who had a brief and unhappy military career, has also been reported seen there.

From the Civil War era comes the ghost of Abraham Lincoln, who also seems to get around a great deal. Ulysses S. Grant may have planned his final campaign at the fort — and his ghost has been spotted, too. The ghosts of both Lincoln and Grant have been reported (appropriately) in the building called Old Quarters Number One, in a room once assigned to house distinguished visitors.

Jefferson Davis, the president of the Confederacy, was imprisoned at Fort Monroe from 1865 to 1867 after the war. His ghost has also been reported at the fort, though not in the guest room. There are also some anonymous ghosts, like that of a little boy who apparently died tragically in one of the fort's homes and returns to throw crockery, move tables, and generally make himself a nuisance to later tenants.

But by far, the most famous of Fort Monroe's ghosts is the Luminous Lady. Though she comes from the Civil War era, she has less to do with war than with that other great staple of ghost stories — love.

During the war, there were some fourteen hundred residents of Fort Monroe. The garrison had easy access to the sea, so they were by no means besieged or cut off from the outside world. Still, they were surrounded by hostile territory, and life inside the moat and walls was very much like life in an isolated town. There was very little real privacy.

One of the officers at the fort was a Captain Wilhelm Kirtz, a rather unimaginative middle-aged member of the Steuben Rifles, a unit made up of German-Americans. Just before the war began he had married a lively young woman named Camille. Right from the start it was a bad match. In addition to being much older than his wife and very dull, Kirtz was also jealous and occasionally violent.

Captain Kirtz was not a monster. He tried to control his jealousy. But in the hothouse atmosphere that existed in Fort Monroe, all the officers and their wives saw one another daily, and Kirtz began to worry that his wife was paying special attention first to one man, and then to another. Every glance, every smile was like a blow to him.

Kirtz flew into jealous rages, where he shouted at his wife, accused her of all manner of things, and occasionally beat her. He was always sorry afterward, but still the rages and the beatings continued.

Up to this point, Camille had done nothing more than a little harmless flirting. But that was to change with the arrival of a handsome young officer named Peter. Oddly, though Captain Kirtz had been suspicious of everyone else, he barely noticed the way Peter looked at his wife, or the way she looked back at him.

At first, the relationship between Camille and the young officer was an innocent one. It had to be. In the tiny Fort Monroe community, Peter and Camille had no chance to be alone so long as Captain Kirtz was around. Then one day, Captain Kirtz was sent on a mission. It wasn't a very important mission, and Kirtz bitterly resented having to take a long and uncomfortable journey on such a trivial matter. But it was an order from his commanding officer, and he had no choice but to obey.

Suddenly an opportunity had opened up. Peter whispered to Camille that they should meet in Matthews Street — not really a street at all but a narrow, dark alley, even darker than usual on that moonless night. This was the first time the two had ever been alone together; it was just for a few moments, but Camille believed that she was deeply in love with the young officer.

Despite its darkness, Matthews Street was still a dangerous meeting place in crowded Fort Monroe. They might easily be seen by anyone. So Peter took the bolder (but he believed safer) step of visiting Camille in her quarters, confident that her husband would be absent for at least another day.

It was a reckless plan. The irritated Colonel Kirtz finished his assignment early and rushed back to the fort, arriving late in the evening a full day before he was expected. He found his wife in the arms of another man.

Captain Kirtz was both enraged and armed. He drew his pistol and fired. He may have intended to kill Peter, but the shot hit his wife. Camille lingered for a few hours, and died before morning.

Captain Kirtz was arrested for his wife's murder. The custom of the day held that this sort of "crime of passion" was not really murder. Kirtz served a prison sentence — though no one seems to know where or for how long.

Years later, Captain Kirtz returned to Fort Monroe for a visit. When he entered the fort, he did not give his real name. It probably would have made no difference if he had. After the mass slaughter of the war, a single killing would have been forgotten. But Kirtz had not forgotten what he had done. He couldn't sleep. He walked aimlessly around the familiar buildings until he found himself in the dark, narrow confines of Matthews Street.

Reward poster for the capture of conspirators John Surratt, John Wilkes Booth, and David Herold.

Union dead on the battlefield at Gettysburg.

Mag. Rathbone.   Miss Harris.   Mrs. Lincoln.   President.   Assassin.

THE ASSASSINATION OF PRESIDENT LINCOLN.

AT FORD'S THEATRE WASHINGTON. D.C. APRIL 14TH 1865.

A Currier & Ives print showing the assassination of President Abraham Lincoln by John Wilkes Booth. On the left are Major Henry Reed Rathbone and his fiancée, Clara Harris. In the center is Mary Todd Lincoln.

Conspirator Louis Powell (also known as Louis Payne), who attacked

Bodies of conspirators Mary Surratt, Louis Powell, David Herold, and George Atzerodt after their hanging in the yard of the old Washington Arsenal Penitentiary on July 7, 1865.

The Andersonville Prison as it appeared in 1865.

The Old Brick Capitol as it looked during the Civil War when it was a prison.

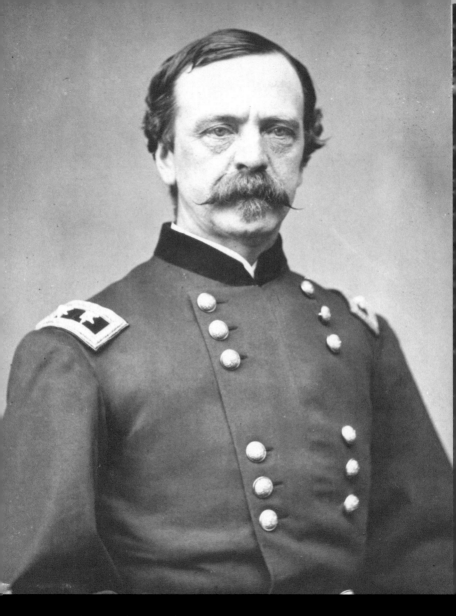

General Daniel Sickles, the one-legged ghost

At the end of the street, he saw a glow, which he first took to be a lantern, but as it got closer he realized that the light came from the figure of a woman. He knew at once what and who this glowing form was.

"Before me stood Camille, as lovely as she had been in life, but instead of the white wraith-like form that I had always associated with apparitions, her limbs and clothing possessed a peculiar and blinding sheen. I placed both hands over my eyes and fell to my knees in the middle of the alleyway."

For the first time, Captain Kirtz recognized his own guilt; he had made his wife's life miserable and may very well have brought about her affair.

When Kirtz uncovered his eyes, the pulsating luminous apparition had disappeared. But he was convinced that it had not been a hallucination or any other sort of trick of the eye or mind. He left the fort, and died a short time later.

Among his effects was a letter describing his experience. It ended: "God forgive me!"

After the story became known, so many others reported seeing the Luminous Lady that she has become, by far, the most famous phantom of ghost-ridden Fort Monroe. Matthews Street, where the glowing form traditionally appears on moonless nights, has been informally renamed Ghost Alley in her honor.

Where to Go
Take Route 64 east toward Norfolk or west toward Williamsburg. Get off at exit 268 and look for Fort Monroe or Casemate Museum signs. The fort has been carefully maintained in its original form.

Please call the site for directions and visiting hours.

Fort Monroe
Hampton, Virginia
(757) 727-2111

Chapter 6

JOHN BROWN—
STILL MARCHING ON

$\mathcal{M}$uch of the old river town of Harpers Ferry looks just as it did in Civil War days. The National Park Service has seen to that. Battered by the war and by floods, Harpers Ferry, Virginia, became virtually a ghost town by the late nineteenth century. But it has been restored since then so that walking the streets of the town today gives visitors a strong and almost eerie feeling of having stepped back in time.

Harpers Ferry is located at the head of the Shenandoah Valley, where the Potomac and Shenandoah Rivers meet, and at the place where Virginia meets West Virginia and Maryland. The town has been, over time, the site of an arsenal, an armory, and a rifle works. George Washington himself had originally selected it as the place for a federal arsenal. Because of its strategic location and its military industry, it was an important Civil War objective for both the North and South. In 1862, Confederate General "Stonewall" Jackson captured Harpers Ferry and took over twelve thousand Union prisoners, the largest surrender of Union forces during the Civil War. But that's not why the town is so famous.

Harpers Ferry will forever be associated with one man — John Brown.

To say that John Brown is a controversial figure in American history is to put the matter as mildly as possible. To some, Brown was a fanatic, a bloodthirsty madman who was ready to sacrifice anyone, including his own sons, to his single-minded vision. To others, he was a saint and a martyr to the antislavery cause.

A tough farmer and a deeply religious man, John Brown had intended to become a minister before he became a fixture in the antislavery or abolitionist movement. With some of his sons (he had twenty children), he became involved in the bloody conflicts between free state and pro-slavery groups in Kansas.

In 1858, Brown convened a remarkable meeting of blacks and whites in Canada. There he declared his intention to set up a stronghold somewhere in Maryland or Virginia where escaped slaves might come and defend themselves. He was to be commander in chief of this theoretical free area.

It was a wildly unrealistic idea, but Brown's vision, strength, and his absolute belief in his cause attracted the attention of a number of wealthy and prominent abolitionists. A group of them agreed to fund the project.

In the summer of 1859, a small, armed band led by Brown set up a kind of military headquarters in a rented farmhouse near Harpers Ferry. There were twenty-two men, six of them either Brown's sons or related to him by marriage. Five were freed or escaped slaves. At their headquarters they planned and trained for a military operation.

To his followers John Brown was an inspiring figure. Tall, strong-featured, taciturn, and with a magnificent flowing beard, he was completely without fear and possessed the unshakable conviction that he was doing God's work. He began each morning by reading a chapter from the Bible.

That is how he began the morning of October 16, 1859. However, on that evening Brown and his tiny army entered Harpers Ferry, easily captured the lightly guarded federal arsenal, and took a number of hostages from among leading men in the area. But Brown had no clear idea of what was going to happen next. He seems to have believed that there would be a general rising among the slaves who would flock to his banner. That never happened.

Brown and his men held out against the small, poorly armed local militia. But then they faced a much more formidable enemy. A company of ninety U.S. Marines under the command of then Colonel Robert E. Lee arrived at Harpers Ferry just before midnight on October 17. In the early hours of October 18, Lee sent his Lieutenant J. E. B. Stuart to the armory fire-engine house, where Brown and his men were holding out, to demand their surrender.

Despite the obvious hopelessness of his situation, John Brown was not about to surrender. The marines battered down the door to the engine house and quickly overwhelmed the tiny group of raiders. Ten were killed in the assault, and Brown himself was seriously wounded.

He was taken to Charlestown, Virginia (now Charles Town, West Virginia), and tried for murder, slave insurrection, and treason. At the trial, there was evidence introduced that some of Brown's relatives and ancestors had been mentally unstable and that Brown himself might suffer from a mental illness. Brown would not permit any insanity plea on his behalf. He acknowledged what he had done and insisted that he was doing God's work. "I believe that to have interfered as I have done — as I have always freely admitted I have done — in behalf of His despised poor, was not wrong but right."

The outcome of the trial was a foregone conclusion. John Brown was convicted, and on December 2, 1859, he was hanged.

As he was being taken from his prison cell to the scaffold, he handed an onlooker this message:

> "I, John Brown, am now quite *certain* that the crimes of the *guilty land will* never be purged *away* but with Blood. I had as I now *think: vainly* flattered myself that without *very* much bloodshed it might be done."

It was a prophetic message, for within two years the Civil War, America's bloodiest conflict, was to begin. And one of the underlying issues was, as it had been for John Brown at Harpers Ferry, slavery.

Among the fifteen hundred who witnessed Brown's execution was future Presidential assassin John

Wilkes Booth, then a member of the Grays, a company of Virginia militia raised in that city.

From any practical or military standpoint, John Brown's raid at Harpers Ferry was an insane act. But Brown believed that his actions might change the course of history, and in a sense they did. Under other circumstances such an act would have been nothing more than an isolated "incident," barely a footnote to history. But in the already tense atmosphere of 1859, it inflamed the passions between slaveholders and abolitionists. For pro-slavery proponents, it raised the specter of their greatest fear — a massive slave insurrection. For abolitionists, it provided a hero and martyr, a godly man willing to die in order to free the slaves.

When the war broke out, many Union troops marched into battle singing the stirring anthem "John Brown's Body," which had been adapted to commemorate him.

The lyrics run, in part:

"John Brown's body lies a-mould'ring in the grave
John Brown's body lies a-mould'ring in the grave

John Brown's body lies a-mould'ring in the
grave
But his soul goes marching on."

John Brown's body is "a-mould'ring" in a grave in
North Elba, New York, where he lived for part of his
life. His soul, or his ghost, appears to be "marching
on" in Harpers Ferry, which will be forever associated
with his name.

Accounts of the sighting of Brown's ghost abound
in the area. As you might imagine from a man of
such strong and indomitable character, his is not a
shy ghost. This ghost does not hide in dark houses at
midnight. John Brown's ghost appears boldly out in
the open when everyone can see him.

Many tourists say that they have seen a tall, stern,
magnificently bearded man in mid-nineteenth-
century clothes striding down the main street in
broad daylight. Assuming that he is a John Brown
impersonator who had been hired to provide a little
local color for visitors, the man is often asked to pose
for pictures. Silently, he agrees and stands there, an
unsmiling figure towering over the smiling tourists.
But when the pictures are developed, the image of
John Brown is never there!

Others have seen John Brown accompanied by his large black dog, walking swiftly along the old storefronts in the center of town. When they reach the fire-engine house, scene of the raiders' last stand, man and dog enter, right through the closed door.

Where to Go
Please call the sites for directions and visiting hours.

Harpers Ferry National Historical Park
Visitors Center, P.O. Box 65
Harpers Ferry, West Virginia
(304)-535-6298

John Brown Farm State Historic Site
John Brown Rd., Lake Placid, New York
(518)-323-3900

Chapter 7

THE ANDERSONVILLE HORROR

*P*risoner-of-war camps are, by their very nature, terrible places. During the Civil War, Andersonville was the worst of all of them. The Andersonville Prison, located a few miles northeast of Americus, Georgia, was the largest of the Southern prison camps for Union soldiers. The physical area of the camp was surprisingly small, covering just about twenty-seven acres. The camp itself was really nothing more than a collection of rude wooden huts and tents surrounded by a heavily guarded stockade. At its height, however, approximately thirty-two thousand prisoners were jammed into the Andersonville prison. Some thirteen thousand of them died there, primarily from disease and malnutrition (although a few were executed or shot by guards for trying to escape or other offenses). Sometimes they died at the rate of 150 a day.

For many years after the war, the Andersonville prison was largely forgotten. Or maybe it would be more accurate to say that memories of the camp were deliberately repressed — we all try to forget things that are too terrible and painful. Many men die on battlefields, yet battlefields are remembered and celebrated because they are also scenes of courage and heroism. At Andersonville, there was only the worst kind of death and suffering. Then, in 1955, the popular author McKinlay Kantor's novel *Andersonville* was published. It became an extraordinary best-seller and won a Pulitzer Prize. Next to *Gone with the Wind*, it is the most popular Civil War novel of all time. More than anything else, Kantor's book dramatically brought the horrors of the mid-nineteenth century to mid-twentieth-century readers.

McKinlay Kantor wrote,

"More than thirty thousand men crowded upon twenty-seven acres of land, with little or no shelter from the intense heat of a Southern summer, or from rain and from the dew of night, with coarse corn bread from which the husk had not been removed, with but scant supplies of fresh meat and vegetables, with little or no attention to hygiene, with festering masses of filth at the very doors of their rude dens and tents. . . ."

Some, particularly Southerners, were deeply offended by the book. They have insisted that the undeniable horrors of Andersonville were not the result of deliberate cruelty but of benign incompetence and the generally desperate conditions that prevailed in the Confederacy during the agonizing final months of the war when the camp was most crowded. The Confederate troops and the general population didn't have adequate food or medical supplies — prisoners of war would inevitably have had the lowest priority. Some people even tried to blame the Union side for conditions at the camp, because the Union was unwilling to exchange prisoners of war and this Union policy may have led to the overcrowding. Others said that Union prisoner camps were nearly as bad. Still, the way the Andersonville prisoners were forced to exist was so terrible that it is impossible to find reasonable excuses for the utterly inhumane conditions that existed at the camp.

A year after the war ended, Andersonville camp commander Captain Henry Wirtz was tried for brutality, convicted, and hanged at the Old Capitol Prison in Washington, D.C. He was the only American ever tried and convicted as a war criminal on American soil.

Some say that Wirtz was incompetent and insensitive, but not really a monster; they believe his trial was a sham, an exercise in revenge rather than justice. Wirtz has defenders, particularly in Andersonville itself. In the town there are two monuments and a small museum devoted to his memory, and he is often referred to as a "hero-martyr." An annual ceremony in his honor is held on November 10, the day of Wirtz's execution. It does not attract many visitors.

After the Civil War, the remains of the notorious prison camp were allowed to rot away, and the area was reclaimed by the forest. Some, like the famous Civil War nurse Clara Barton, tried to have Andersonville made a national shrine, but the plan never got off the ground. Andersonville was nearly forgotten, as many people thought it should be. But the tremendous interest inspired by McKinlay Kantor's novel resulted in the area's designation as the Andersonville National Historic Site — Prison Park and National Cemetery in 1970.

As it looks today, the site does little to convey the real horror of the camp, and the exhibits in the museums are devoted to American prisoners in all wars.

Still the spirits of the dead linger and they do recall the horrors of the camp. Captain Wirtz has become, in legend at least, one of the many ghosts associated with Andersonville. His restless spirit has been reported walking down the road that leads to the Andersonville National Historic Site — perhaps condemned to revisit the terrible place eternally.

Many visitors report hearing strange moans and shrieks or seeing indistinct figures in the fog, which might or might not be the ghosts of men who died there.

Stories like this are common and inevitable at battlefields, prisons, major accident sites, practically anywhere that is associated with mass and violent death. But one account truly stands out among the many vague tales.

The strange event took place in July 1990, and

was reported by two men who were touring the South, visiting as many Civil War historical sites as they could during a two-week vacation. They had arrived at the Andersonville site when darkness was already beginning to fall. Instead of going to the campground, which they figured would be full, they simply parked their van outside the cemetery gates and prepared to sleep in the back. The area was deserted at night, and they didn't believe they would be breaking any laws.

One of the men fell asleep immediately. But the other man was restless and sat up reading, using a tiny battery-operated lamp. Shortly after midnight, a breeze sprang up and the man who had been reading became aware of a strong and unpleasant odor that got stronger and more unpleasant by the moment.

At first, he thought that something left in the back of the van had begun to rot. He searched around using his reading lamp but found nothing. And the smell was still getting stronger. The man slid back the door of the van so that he could step outside for a breath of fresh air. But it was no use — the smell outside was overpowering.

The odor made him feel like throwing up. But there was also something strangely familiar about it.

Then he remembered his tour of duty in Vietnam. The odor reminded him of what it smelled like in a military field hospital in the jungle heat. But this was much, much worse.

Then came sounds, indistinct at first, but like the faint murmurs of men's voices.

By this time his friend was awakened by the overpowering smell. "Where's it coming from?" he asked.

"I don't know. It's all around us," the first man said.

It had rained earlier in the evening, and one of the men reached down to put his hand in a puddle that had formed on the ground. He sniffed at his fingers and the smell struck him with the force of a physical blow. The odor seemed to have been released from the ground by the rain; it was strongest in the puddles.

Then, abruptly, both the odor and the noises began to fade, and within a few minutes they were entirely gone.

The next morning, the two men talked to some park employees. They were told that after nearly a century and a quarter, any odors that would have been associated with the cemetery or the prison camp itself would surely have long since disappeared.

The park employees could offer no explanation for the strange experience — no natural explanation, that is — at all.

Where to Go
Please call the site for directions and visiting hours.

Andersonville National Historic Site —
 Prison Park and National Cemetery
Nine miles northeast of Americus, Georgia, on
 Highway 49
Andersonville, Georgia
(912)-924-0343

Chapter 8

THE LADY IN BLACK

*F*ort Warren is a grim-looking example of nineteenth-century massive military architecture. It is located on Georges Island in Boston Harbor, seven nautical miles from downtown Boston.

During the Civil War, the fort was used as a prison and held many Confederate soldiers. It had a sinister reputation and was known as the Northern Bastille or the Corridor of Dungeons, a prison from which escape was thought to be nearly impossible.

Today the old fort is a popular tourist attraction. Tens of thousands of visitors have walked the Corridor of Dungeons and have listened to the caretaker recount the fort's grim history, particularly the tragic tale of the Lady in Black.

As the story comes to an end, the narrator will stoop down and swing back the cover of a casket on the floor. Immediately a figure, wearing a black dress and a hat with a thick veil, leaps out with a blood-curdling scream.

Of course, the black-clad figure is just a young woman or a small man dressed up for the occasion. But it is a performance that the visitor is not likely to forget.

The story of the Lady in Black began in the early days of the war. Andrew Lanier of Crawfordville, Georgia, was called to fight for the Confederacy. He married his longtime sweetheart on June 28, 1861, just before he left. Two days later, he marched north to battle, and within two months he had been captured and sent to Fort Warren.

While it was difficult, and some believed nearly impossible to escape from the island prison, there were many Southern sympathizers, even in the Boston area. In some ways, the prison leaked like a sieve. Letters from Confederate prisoners were regularly carried from the prison and passed southward.

Andrew Lanier wrote a letter to his young bride, telling of his capture, his incarceration, and his terrible loneliness. This sad and moving letter was eventually received by his wife in Georgia.

Oddly, though the story is well-known, the young woman's first name has not come down to us. She is known only as Mrs. Andrew Lanier, and is most frequently referred to as "the girl." This is a shame, because she seems to have been a remarkable individual: As soon as she learned of her husband's fate, for instance, she determined to go to Boston and find some way to free him.

She first made contact with a blockade runner who agreed, for a fee, to take her up the coast to Cape Cod, Massachusetts. Mrs. Lanier had her hair cut short and obtained a suit of men's clothes and an old pepperbox pistol. Two and a half months later the "young man" was put ashore on Cape Cod. She had in her possession the names of several Confederate sympathizers who would help her. Within a week, she was able to establish herself at a home in Hull, Massachusetts, less than a mile away from Georges Island. She studied the fortification through a telescope until she had familiarized herself with the prison layout and routine.

On the stormy night of January 15, 1862, Mrs. Lanier's sympathetic host rowed her to the island and left her on the beach. She carried with her a bundle that held her pistol and a short-handled pick. Because her movements were obscured by the storm, she was able to get close to the walls of the prison. Everyone inside seemed to be asleep.

She then whistled a tune that she and her husband had once used to signal each other. At first, there was no response. She repeated the tune several times louder and louder. Finally, an answering whistle came from the fort.

Looking up, she saw that there was a row of narrow slits in the granite wall of the fortress. In time of attack, guns would have been pushed through the slits. Now, she saw a rope being lowered from one of them. It came low enough so that she could just grab the end of it.

"Hang on," a voice cried. In a moment, she was being pulled up, bundle and all. Being small and thin, she was just able to squeeze through the narrow slit. Waiting on the other side was her husband, Andrew Lanier.

At the time, there were about six hundred Confederate prisoners inside Fort Warren. They had been planning an escape by digging a short tunnel out of the prison to the beach and boarding a ship they hoped Southern sympathizers would provide for them.

With the unexpected arrival of the girl with a digging tool and a gun, they decided to try a bolder plan. They would dig a tunnel to the parade ground inside the fort. There they would overwhelm the small garrison of eighty or so Union soldiers and seize the arsenal. Then they would turn the guns of the fort against Boston. It was a crazy plan but the prisoners were able to convince themselves that it would work and even change the course of the war to ensure a Confederate victory.

The tunneling went on for weeks, with prisoners carrying away the dirt in their jackets or small containers to conceal what they were doing. Finally the leaders of the attempt believed that the tunnel had reached the center of the parade ground.

They planned their breakout for one o'clock in the morning when most of the guards would be sleeping. But as a young lieutenant swung the pick for what should have been the final thrust into the open air, he heard the sickening sound of metal striking granite. The tunnelers had miscalculated badly. Instead of ending the tunnel in the middle of the parade ground, they had dug it to the wall of the keep, the innermost and most strongly fortified building within the fortress.

The sound of the pick striking rock alerted the

sentries, who guessed what was happening. Almost immediately, the entire Union garrison was on alert.

Colonel Justin Dimmock, commanding officer of Fort Warren, ordered an inspection of the Corridor of Dungeons. Evidence of the digging was soon discovered, but when the roll was called, eleven prisoners were found to be missing.

Colonel Dimmock shouted down to those still in the tunnel, "You have failed, so you might as well come out and surrender."

Slowly eleven Southerners crawled out of the shaft. The last to emerge was Andrew Lanier. With all the prisoners accounted for, the guards relaxed for a moment. And just then the girl, whose existence the guards had never suspected, sprang out of the tunnel waving her gun.

"I've a pistol and I know how to use it!" she shouted.

After a moment, Colonel Dimmock regained his composure. He raised his hands and advanced toward the girl. But as he did so, he signaled his men to follow. They formed a circle around her. Then, with a sudden motion of his arm, the colonel tried to knock the pistol out of her hand. She fired, but the pistol was old and rusty. It exploded, and one fragment of metal flew through the skull of Andrew Lanier, killing him instantly.

The Confederate soldier's body was buried in a cemetery in the fort. A week later, his widow was sentenced to be executed as a spy.

On the morning of February 2, 1862, one of the guards asked Mrs. Lanier if she had any final request, for she was to be hanged in an hour. She replied, "Why yes, I'm tired of wearing this suit of men's clothes. I'd like to put on a gown before I die."

There weren't any fashionable women's clothes to be found at the fort. The only thing that turned up were some black robes left over from a theatrical performance the summer before. Mrs. Andrew Lanier was hanged in that costume. Her body was then cut down and buried beside her husband's.

One of those who had witnessed the hanging was Private Richard Cassidy, and seeing a woman hung preyed on his mind, particularly since he had been given the duty of patrolling the spot where the hanging had taken place. The other soldiers kidded him and warned him to watch out for the Lady in Black. He tried to laugh it off, but somehow he couldn't.

Then one night, seven weeks after the execution, Private Cassidy ran into the guardhouse, screaming incoherently. It was over an hour before he was calm enough to relate what had happened. He said that he was walking his post thinking about the execution when suddenly two hands came out of the dark and grabbed him around the throat. At first, he didn't realize who or what had attacked him. But he squirmed and struggled until he faced his attacker — it was the Lady in Black. That extra shock gave him enough strength to break free, escape the ghostly clutches, and run to the guardhouse.

The other guards simply laughed at his story. But his superior officers didn't think it was so funny. They sentenced him to thirty days in the guardhouse for deserting his post.

But Private Cassidy wasn't the only one to see the mysterious black-clad figure. Years later, in the winter of 1891, four officers walking through the fresh snow saw the footprints made by a woman's slippers. Since there was no woman living at the fort at that time, the officers assumed they had been made by the Lady in Black. This was long after the remains of the unfortunate Lanier and his wife had been dug up and returned to their hometown for final burial.

The most serious encounter with the Lady in Black took place during World War II. The sentry who was patrolling the area of the execution went completely mad while on duty, and never recovered his senses.

During World War II, Fort Warren housed not only military men but their families as well. During that period, there were numerous sightings of the Lady in Black, particularly by army wives.

Author Edward Rowe Snow, who led a successful campaign to preserve Fort Warren, found a photograph of a group of soldiers taken at the fort in 1862. Standing at the rear of the group is the indistinct figure of a woman dressed in black. But no women were staying at the fort at that time. Snow thought that the photograph might show the ghost of the Lady in Black.

After the end of World War II, Fort Warren's military usefulness came to an end. In 1946, it was opened to the general public and reported sightings of the Lady in Black have declined since then — except, of course, if you happen to be one of those who see her jump out of her coffin during a tour.

Where to Go

Historic Fort Warren on Georges Island can be reached by ferry from Boston during the summer months.

Please call the site for directions and visiting hours.

Fort Warren
A forty-five minute ferry ride from Long Wharf in Boston
Georges Island, Massachusetts
(617)-328-3900

Chapter 9

THE REENACTORS

*I*magine this: You are walking through a famous Civil War battlefield, reading the historical markers and trying to imagine what it was like there nearly a century and a half ago.

Then, quite suddenly, you hear the sound of gunfire. You turn around and see, through a haze of gunsmoke and dust, a crowd of men in familiar gray uniforms, carrying rifles with fixed bayonets and running toward you, screaming.

Did you step through a hole in time? Are you watching a ghostly repeat of Pickett's Charge?

Probably not.

It is far more likely that you have stumbled into the middle of a Civil War reenactment.

There has always been a small number of Civil War buffs who would put on period uniforms and stage the occasional reenactment of a Civil War battle. But interest in this sort of activity has grown over the past decade. There are now tens of thousands of "reenactors" who will spend large sums of money for authentic-looking uniforms and weapons. They will travel great distances and endure heat, rain, mud, mosquitoes, and lots of other discomforts to take part in a mock battle.

For the sereous reenactor, this isn't just dressing up for a day and playing at war. Most are extremely dedicated and knowledgeable. The growing hobby of Civil War reenacting is a genuine attempt to duplicate the look, feel, sound, and occasionally the smell of the actual event. The "hardcore" reenactors (they prefer to be called "living historians") will put on dreadfully uncomfortable Civil War uniforms, authentic right down to the underwear. They will spend days sleeping out in the open, just as the real soldiers did nearly a century and a half ago, and eat nothing but hard biscuits and salt pork, the common soldier's diet of the day while in the field. One writer commented, "I would as soon tramp barefoot through a snake-infested Ecuadorian marsh as spend a week in a period costume." Most "hardcores" are Southerners. Some will diet themselves into rail thinness so they can more closely match the gaunt look of most underfed Confederate soldiers. These folks are really serious.

Sometimes the reenactors look so authentic that even the ghosts become confused. That's apparently what happened at the Fort Pulaski National Monument in Savannah, Georgia.

Fort Pulaski was built in the 1830s to guard the approach up the Savannah River from the ocean to the city. The fort was named after Revolutionary War hero Casimir Pulaski. It was considered a vital coastal fortification and the Georgia militia took over the fort even before that state seceded from the Union. However, Fort Pulaski soon proved to be a dubious prize for the South.

The reason was that, in the thirty years after the fort was completed, artillery had been greatly improved. That meant that the brick fort could no longer stand up against the kind of firepower that the Union troops possessed. Early in 1862, the Union Army built an artillery battery on an island two miles from the fort. The four-hundred-man garrison at Fort Pulaski didn't have the manpower to assault the

Union position, and their guns were not powerful enough to reach it. The newly installed Union artillery, however, was powerful enough to reach the walls of Fort Pulaski. Union commander General David Hunter asked for the fort's surrender, but Confederate commander Colonel Charles H. Olmstead refused. The Union batteries opened fire on the morning of April 10, 1862, and by nightfall much of the fort's wall had been reduced to a pile of shattered bricks.

By the following day, Olmstead realized that a few well-placed shots could hit the fort's munitions magazine — then the entire fort, and everyone in it, would be destroyed. And there was not a thing that he could do about it — except surrender. By two P.M. of April 11 that's exactly what he did, even though just one of the defenders had been killed in the bombardment.

Surrender was the only sensible course of action. But surrender, no matter how necessary and wise, is usually not remembered kindly. And the charming old city of Savannah is alive (if one can use such a phrase in this context) with ghosts. It would be very surprising if the nearby fort had remained unhaunted. The ghosts of Fort Pulaski have a special poignancy, for they are said to return eternally to their posts, seeking some sort of redemption for their surrender. Many visitors to the Fort Pulaski National Monument have reported encounters with phantom defenders, but one encounter in the late 1980s was unique.

The Civil War film *Glory* (released in 1989) was filmed in the Savannah area, and a large number of Civil War reenactors were used as extras. Nine of the reenactors stopped off at the fort on their way to the filming. They were wearing Confederate uniforms.

They saw a young man in the uniform of a Confederate lieutenant, and assuming he was another reenactor, they waved at him and gave him a friendly nod.

The young man's response was surprising. He ordered them to halt and demanded that they give a proper salute, since he was a superior officer.

One of the reenactors was offended. "Who does he think he is?" he asked. "We ain't on the set yet."

The lieutenant got angry. He didn't seem to know what they were talking about. He said their insolence would not be tolerated, but nothing could be done at the moment because a Yankee attack was imminent. Then he shouted, "Attention! About-face!" with such force and conviction that the nine men lined up and did exactly what he had ordered.

They waited for the next order. But it never came. And when they turned around, they found that the arrogant young lieutenant had vanished.

They searched around and never found any trace of him. They never found him among the other reenactors on the film set, either.

The reenactors finally decided that they had met a ghost. "If he wasn't a ghost," one of them laughed, "we'd sure like to hear from him. That was one good-looking uniform he had on."

Pickett's Mill near Dallas, Georgia, is a popular site for reenactors. Though the battle fought there in 1864 is not a particularly famous one, the site itself is extraordinarily well preserved and a program in which the battle is reenacted is held every year on or near the May 27 date on which the battle was actually fought.

A high point of the battle for those taking part is the charge of Confederate General Hiram Granbury's Texas brigade. The Texans had trapped a large number of Union troops in a ravine. Though outnumbered and poorly positioned, the Union troops were resisting bravely. But at about ten in the evening, the Texans fixed their bayonets and came charging down the slope, giving a rousing rebel yell. Overwhelmed, the surviving Union troops surrendered and the battle was over.

During one reenactment, a couple of the participants arrived late in the evening of the day before the program was to take place. It was raining hard, and the men (obviously not hardcore reenactors) decided that they didn't want to set up their tent in the darkness and mud at the campsite about half a mile away. So they just pulled into the parking lot at the visitors' center, rolled out their blankets, and went to sleep in the back of the truck. The visitors' center was located very near the ravine where the Texans' final charge took place.

Around two A.M., they were awakened by noises. They couldn't quite make them out but they thought they heard a herd of deer or other large animals moving around in the ravine. Then they heard a noise that they were very familiar with — the high-pitched rebel yell, followed by the footsteps of men running down the hill.

They decided that somebody must have gotten so excited that they started the performance a day early. The noises stopped, and the two men went back to sleep.

Early the next morning, they walked over to the ravine, still muddy from the previous night's rain.

They expected to find it all trampled up. Instead they found nothing — no footprints at all, no sign that anyone had run down the hill yelling. When they got to the campsite, their friends swore that there had been no impromptu reenactment of the Texans' charge.

No one had been in the ravine that night. No one living, at least.

Where to Go
Please call the sites for directions and visiting hours.

Fort Pulaski National Monument
Savannah, Georgia
(912) 786-5787

Pickett's Mill Historic Site
26409 Mount Tabor Road
Dallas, Georgia
(770) 443-7850

Chapter 10

THREE STRANGE TALES

$\mathcal{T}$he Washington, D.C., building known as the Old Brick Capitol served as a temporary home for Congress after the British burned the Capitol during the War of 1812. Later it was converted to residences, and during the Civil War, it was used as a federal prison.

In 1922, the building became the headquarters of the National Women's Party, which had led the drive to get the vote for women. In addition to the headquarters for the movement, the building contained a dormitory for many who worked for the party.

By that time the building itself had not housed any prisoners or witnessed any executions for over fifty years. The cells had been converted into bedrooms, and all obvious traces of its grim past as a Civil War prison had been eliminated. Still, the ghosts lingered.

Women who had stayed in the building recounted all manner of odd noises, strange sightings, and other unexplained incidents. Sometimes at night, for instance, they would hear the clank of a long-vanished cell door being slammed shut.

There was, of course, the ghost of Mary Surratt, who spent her last days in the prison. She could not only be seen at the window but could be heard weeping as well.

The women decided the sound of someone pacing back and forth was the ghost of the Andersonville prison commander Henry Wirtz. He also spent his last days in the Old Brick Capitol before he was taken out to the courtyard and hanged.

There was the ghostly, bitter female laughter that many speculated must have been the spirit of Belle Boyd, a notorious Confederate spy. After she was captured, she spent many unhappy months imprisoned in the Old Brick Capitol.

And then there was the music. One of the women staying in the building played the violin. She kept the instrument hanging on the wall of the parlor, though she was so busy that she seldom played.

Then one evening, some of the women heard violin music coming from the parlor. They assumed that the violinist had decided to give a rare performance. But when they went down to the parlor to enjoy the music, they found that the room was empty, and the violin hung on the wall in its usual place. The music, however, continued. The house was searched but no violinist was found. They even checked outside to see if someone were trying to play a trick on them. Nobody could find anything to explain the music.

Later in the evening, after the music had stopped, the women discussed the incident. The younger women could not recognize the tune that was being played. Some of the older women, however, recalled the melody. They said it was a favorite from Civil War times. In their childhood, they had heard some of the old veterans humming it. It was the sort of tune with which Confederate prisoners in the Old Brick Capitol would have been familiar.

The women were never able to discover the origin of the music, even though the old melody was heard throughout the building on several different occasions.

Like the sobs, laughter, and footsteps, the Civil War music was regarded as another ghostly manifestation in that most haunted of Washington buildings.

America's Civil War sites attract tourists from around the country and all parts of the world. Is it possible that one of these visitors is himself a ghost?

Visitors to the Stonewall Cemetery, the Confederate section of Mount Hebron Cemetery in Winchester, Virginia, have from time to time reported catching a glimpse of a figure who looks out of place in today's world. The figure is always seen at a distance, and by the time the visitors get close to him they find that he has somehow disappeared.

The description of the figure is always the same: a man of middle height and build with a ramrod-straight military bearing. He wears a long gray military-style greatcoat, and a military-style peaked cap with an insignia on the front that no one has ever been able to see clearly. He looks European rather than American. The man is clearly a soldier, but from some war later than the Civil War.

The most widely accepted identification for this figure is that it is the ghost of the World War II German General Erwin Rommel. Rommel, known as the Desert Fox, has always been the most well-known of Germany's World War II generals. Not only was he an extremely skilled commander, but he was also part of an unsuccessful 1944 plot to assassinate Adolf Hitler and bring the war to a close. When the plot failed, Rommel swallowed poison rather than stand trial.

But what in this world, or the next, would account for the ghost of a World War II German general visiting an American Civil War cemetery? Oddly, there is a genuine connection.

In 1937, before World War II began, a group of German officers visited the United States. They spent some time at the U.S. Army War college in Carlisle, Pennsylvania, and they toured a number of Civil War battlefields. One of the group was the then-obscure Major Erwin Rommel.

Like most students of military history, Rommel was interested in the American Civil War, which is regarded as the first really modern war in history. While in America, Rommel and other German officers visited the area of Winchester, Virginia, site of some of General Stonewall Jackson's most important battles. There is no record that Rommel actually visited the Stonewall Cemetery. (Who would have kept records of the travels of an unknown German officer in 1937?) But he certainly might have visited the cemetery, since it's located on part of a Civil War battleground.

There is, however, another and even more interesting connection. The ghostly figure is always seen near a large tombstone that bears the inscription THE PATTON BROTHERS. It is the gravesite for Colonel Waller Tazwell Patton, killed at Gettysburg in 1863, and his younger brother Colonel George Smith Patton, who was mortally wounded at the battle of Third Winchester in 1864.

Now here's the connection. The most famous member of the Patton family was twentieth-century General George S. Patton, Jr., named after his Civil War grandfather. General Patton, a fierce warrior, was known to his men as "Old Blood and Guts." Though Generals Patton and Rommel never faced each other in the deserts of North Africa, each man had a grudging respect for the other's military skills.

The tale of the ghost of a German general visiting the grave of his adversary's ancestors is one that General Patton himself would have found very appealing. He was a great believer in reincarnation and thought that in previous lives he had been, among other things, a centurian in Caesar's legions and a cavalry officer in Napoleon's army.

It is fitting that former Mississippi Congressman and Confederate Brigadier General William Barksdale would be known in ghost lore primarily for his dog.

Barksdale was mortally wounded while leading his brigade at Gettysburg on July 2, 1863. His body was buried on Hummelbaugh's farm, near the field hospital in which he died.

After the battle, hundreds of people from both the North and the South came to Gettysburg hoping to find a husband, son, brother, or some other missing loved one among the thousands of wounded who had been left behind. Others came to claim the body of one of those killed and take it home for burial.

Among those who came to Gettysburg was Barksdale's widow. She was accompanied by the general's favorite hunting dog. As the dog was led near his master's grave, he began to howl mournfully, as only a hound can do. The dog then planted itself firmly beside the grave and refused to be moved. Even after Barksdale's remains were exhumed and carried away, the dog would not abandon his vigil. Mrs. Barksdale tried everything she could to get the dog to return with her, but nothing worked. Sadly, she returned to Mississippi with her husband's remains, but without his faithful dog.

The dog stayed by his master's former gravesite. People in the area were touched by the animal's loyalty, and they put food out for it. But the dog ate practically nothing, and within a few days it was found dead next to the grave.

Then the rumors began. If you go near the Hummelbaugh farm at midnight on July 2, the date on which Barksdale was fatally shot, you will hear the most bloodcurdling and unearthly howl you can imagine. People said that Barksdale's faithful hound is still there, guarding his master's gravesite and awaiting his return.

The Hummelbaugh farm is certainly still there, though it is now owned by the U.S. Park Service and is home for the park ranger and his family. From time to time, Civil War (and ghost) buffs will hold a July 2 all-night vigil near the farm, to see if they can hear the faithful spectral hound still pining for the return of his long-dead master.

Where to Go

The Old Brick Capitol in Washington is long gone, replaced by the new Supreme Court building.

102

But writer and Washington ghost authority John Alexander notes, "Some say that if the time is right, and the moonbeams are glancing off the marble just a certain way, you may be able to see an apparition of the Old Brick Capitol shimmering before the building that dared to replace it. Some say the air develops a stale musty odor, and sometimes sobs, cries, and the distant clank of a cell door can be heard—if you hang around long enough."

Please call the sites for directions and visiting hours.

Gettysburg National Military Park
96 Taneytown Road
Gettysburg, Pennsylvania
(717) 334-1124

Stonewall Cemetery
305 East Boscawen Street
Winchester, Virginia
(540) 662-4868

Supreme Court
First Street and Maryland Avenue NE
Washington, D.C.
(202) 479-3000

Selected
Bibliography

Alexander, John. *Ghosts: Washington's Most Famous Ghost Stories*. Washington, D.C.: Washingtonian Books, 1975.

Gallagher, Trish. *Ghosts and Haunted Houses of Maryland*. Centreville, MD: Tidewater Publishers, 1988.

Jones, Louis C. *Things That Go Bump in the Night*. Syracuse, NY: Syracuse University Press, 1983.

McNeil, W.K. (editor). *Ghost Stories From the American South*. New York: Dell, 1988.

Norman, Michael and Beth Scott. *Haunted America*. New York: Tor Books, 1994.

Roberts, Nancy, *Civil War Ghost Stories*. Columbia, South Carolina: University of South Carolina Press, 1992.

Smith, Frank (editor). *Phantom Army of the Civil War and Other Southern Ghost Stories*. St. Paul, Minnesota: Llewellyn Publishers, 1997.

Smith, Susy. *Prominent American Ghosts*. New York: World, 1967.

Stevens, Austin N. (editor). *Mysterious New England*. Dublin, New Hampshire: Yankee Publishing, 1971.

Toney, Keith. *Battlefield Ghosts*. Barryville, Virginia: Rockridge Publishing Co., 1997.

Windham, Kathryn Tucker. *Thirteen Mississippi Ghosts and Jeffrey*. Tuscaloosa, Alabama: University of Alabama Press, 1974.

—— and Margaret Gillis Figh. *Thirteen Alabama Ghosts and Jeffrey*. Tuscaloosa, Alabama: University of Alabama Press, 1969.

About the Author

Daniel Cohen is the author of over 160 nonfiction books for adults and young readers. The subjects have ranged from cloning to professional wrestling. He is best known for his books on the bizarre and supernatural. His Scholastic titles include The Alien Files 1, *Contact*; The Alien Files 2, *Conspiracy*; *Real Vampires*; *Young Ghosts*; *Railway Ghosts and Highway Horrors*.

Mr. Cohen is a native of Chicago and former managing editor of *Science Digest* magazine. He and his wife, also a writer, have collaborated on a number of books. They live in Cape May, New Jersey, in a house haunted only by cats and dogs.